Anonymous

Memorial Addresses on the Life and Character of John B. Rice

Anatiposi

Anonymous

Memorial Addresses on the Life and Character of John B. Rice

Reprint of the original, first published in 1875.

1st Edition 2023 | ISBN: 978-3-38282-812-7

Anatiposi Verlag is an imprint of Outlook Verlagsgesellschaft mbH.

Verlag (Publisher): Outlook Verlag GmbH, Zeilweg 44, 60439 Frankfurt, Deutschland
Vertretungsberechtigt (Authorized to represent): E. Roepke, Zeilweg 44, 60439 Frankfurt, Deutschland
Druck (Print): Books on Demand GmbH, In de Tarpen 42, 22848 Norderstedt, Deutschland

EULOGIES.

JOHN B. RICE,
OF ILLINOIS.

ALVAH CROCKER,
OF MASSACHUSETTS.

SAMUEL F. HERSEY,
OF MAINE.

SAMUEL HOOPER,
OF MASSACHUSETTS.

MEMORIAL ADDRESSES

ON THE

Life and Character

OF

JOHN B. RICE,

(A REPRESENTATIVE FROM ILLINOIS,)

DELIVERED IN THE

Senate and House of Representatives,

FEBRUARY 20, 1875.

PUBLISHED BY ORDER OF CONGRESS.

FORTY-THIRD CONGRESS, SECOND SESSION.

1875.

ADDRESSES

ON THE

DEATH OF JOHN B. RICE,

and he did not take his seat at the commencement of the present session, and gradually failing, died as I have stated.

But recently he whom we now mourn was among us in robust health, giving promise of many years of usefulness. His great heart has ceased to beat, and he sleeps the sleep that knows no waking.

We stand above his honored grave and recall the graces and grand qualities of his life.

A good man has gone to rest and the world is poorer for his loss, though richer and better because he once lived.

To those who knew him as he was known here, no word of mine

can add anything to the incense which envelops his memory or increase the respect which in life his high character challenged from all who came in contact with him.

Without pretension, he was industrious, earnest, and able; without obstinacy, he was firm; without self-righteousness, he was scrupulously honest and conscientious in all things; faithful to his friends, yet just to his opponents; true to his convictions, yet ever ready to receive suggestions and advice. Scorning deceit, he diligently sought for truth; fearless in action and in the expression of his own opinions, yet attentive and respectful to those with whom he differed; public-spirited as a citizen, charitable to the needy, sympathetic with the suffering. A gentle, loving, and indulgent father, genial as an associate, he was a man to be honored and loved as he was in life, and sincerely mourned as he is in death.

His early life was not spent under the most auspicious circumstances, and his eminence in his profession, in the social world, and in politics was achieved by his own strong will and sturdy efforts.

JOHN BLAKE RICE was born in the village of Easton, Talbot County, Md., in 1809. His father was a shoemaker, and he learned that trade. It is not known how long he worked at this humble calling, nor is it certain that he might not have continued at it many years longer and the whole current of his life have run in a different channel but for an accidental circumstance something in this wise: The manager of a Baltimore theater, while strolling along one of the streets of the Maryland metropolis one day, overheard a rich musical voice trolling out a song inside a shop. He stopped and listened for a moment and then passed on, but the voice impressed him as unusually fine, and he made it convenient soon after to drop in at that shop and find out the possessor of the fine baritone. After a brief negotiation, the young mechanic was engaged as a chorister in Clemens's Theater, and it was there the stage life of JOHN B. RICE began. This was in 1836. The following year found him a member of the company of the Walnut Street Theater, Philadelphia, where he was engaged for "singing parts," and occasionally was on for a song between acts. While in Philadelphia he married Miss Mary Ann Warren, daughter of the old manager and actor, William Warren, long since deceased. Miss Warren was then playing *soubrette* parts at the Walnut Street Theater. Mr. RICE subsequently went to Albany, N. Y., where he opened the National Amphitheater. That undertaking, however, proved a failure, and he became associated with the proprietor of the Albany Museum. He remained there four or five years as manager, and thence went to Buffalo, where he joined the company of the Eagle Street Theater. He became manager. It was at the Eagle Street Theater in Buffalo, and under Mr. RICE's management, that Dan Marble made his first great hit as a comedian; and it was also here that Charlotte Cushman, then a young lady of twenty-one or twenty-two, played one of her very first star engagements. The Eagle-street enterprise succeeded but moderately in a financial way, and the manager concluded to give it up and go west.

Early in 1847 he went to Milwaukee and there managed a theater for a time. He ascertained that a canal convention—that was an age of canals—was to be held at Chicago in July of that year, 1847. It occurred to Manager RICE to seize the occasion and turn it to account, and with such capital and credit as he could command he went to Chicago and put up a wooden theater on Randolph street between Dearborn and State streets. He had calculated rightly; the canal convention brought a large number of strangers to the city, and the theater made money rapidly until it burned down.

The first "star" introduced to the Chicago public under his management was Edwin Forrest, who appeared as Jack Cade, June 15, 1847.

Two months after the destruction of the wooden theater on Randolph street, Mr. RICE purchased a lot on Dearborn street, the present site of Rice's Block, and in the month following (September 16) the foundation for a new theater was laid. It was opened February 3, 1851. This theater was prosperous, and in the subsequent years " stars " of the first magnitude played within its walls. Charlotte Cushman was the most prominent.

In February, 1857, Mr. RICE, having accumulated considerable wealth, decided to retire from the business. His management practically ended November 27, 1857, when the season closed. He determined to utilize his property by turning it into business places. This was done, and was occupied as stores and offices until 1871, when it was destroyed in the great fire. A substantial structure was erected on the site the following year, and is known as " Rice's Block," a monument of his enterprise and faith in the future of his loved city.

After abandoning the theater Mr. RICE devoted himself to the improvement of his real estate, of which he had acquired considerable. During all the time he managed a stage there was never allowed anything which would tinge the cheek of the most refined with a blush.

Although a prominent and active citizen almost from the day of his arrival in Chicago, and a warm republican from the day of the organization of that party, Mr. RICE took no great part in political life until 1865, when he was nominated as the candidate of the " Union party " for mayor, and elected by a large majority. In 1867 he was renominated by acclamation, and again elected by a large majority. When his term of office expired in the fall of 1869, he refused to be a candidate for re-election. His two administrations were singularly fortunate. There were no jobs in the council and no complaints of indifference on the part of the mayor. As presiding officer of the council he was in all respects the best that body has ever had. He took an active part in every detail of the city affairs, and was thoroughly conversant with all its necessities.

From 1869 to 1872 he took no active part in politics; but in the fall of the latter year, when the republicans of the new first congressional district wanted a candidate, he was unanimously selected as the representative of his party. He was chosen by an immense majority, swollen by his own personal strength, and went to Washington to discharge his new duties, bearing with him the same conscientious determination to fulfill the high functions of his office that he had displayed in other and less important positions. His record in Congress is well known. A new member, busied in learning details, he had few opportunities of displaying the real ability which was in him; but when he spoke and acted it was always wisely and well. By his associates he was loved and respected.

By his death, which occurred in almost the prime of his life, the first congressional district has lost its first Representative, the city and county one of its best citizens, and his family a kind and affectionate father.

Mr. RICE's family consisted of one son and five daughters. His son enlisted early in the war, and was killed at Chickamauga, Tenn., September 19, 1863, while in command of Company A of the Eightyninth Illinois Volunteers. His daughters all are living; and they, and his wife, who also survives him, mourn him as only such can mourn for such a husband and father.

In the city where he lived, and over which he had so long, so acceptably, and so justly ruled, and where he was so well and widely known, he was most appreciated and loved. The announcement of his death carried sorrow to every household there; few men ever had or ever will win as he had won the hearts of all—the high and low, the rich and poor alike of that city. And we shall be fortunate indeed if, when our work is done, it has been as good and our lives as pure as that of him of whom we take the last good-by to·day.

I submit the following resolutions:

Resolved, That this House has heard with deep regret of the death

of Hon. JOHN B. RICE, a member of this House from the State of
Illinois.

Resolved, That, as a testimony of respect to his memory the officers
and members of this House will wear the usual badge of mourning
for the space of thirty days.

Resolved, That a copy of these resolutions be transmitted by the
Clerk to the family of the deceased.

ADDRESS OF MR. CORWIN, OF ILLINOIS.

Mr. SPEAKER: After listening to the eloquent remarks of my colleague [Mr. WARD] I do not rise to pronounce a formal eulogy upon
the late JOHN B. RICE, but simply to add my tribute of respect to
the memory of one who was my esteemed friend.

Although I had on one or two occasions prior to the assembling
of this Congress met Hon. JOHN B. RICE, my acquaintance with
him only commenced when we met in this Hall in December, 1873.
In the selection of seats at the commencement of this Congress it so
happened that we were placed at adjoining desks, and continued to
occupy contiguous seats during the long, protracted session of seven
months. Sitting side by side and representing districts almost
adjoining in the same State very naturally led to frequent conversa-
tions and an interchange of opinions upon the various questions that
came before the House. As our acquaintance improved this interchange of thought and opinion became more and more frank and
unreserved until, long before the close of the session, our conversa-
tions were characterized by the fullest confidence and all the freedom
of warm friendship. It was in this unreserved intercourse, in the
expression of his matured opinions as well as in his impromptu suggestions, I had the amplest opportunities to discover the more
striking characteristics of the deceased, and learned to respect his
many noble qualities both of mind and heart.

As we have been informed by the gentleman who preceded me, Mr. RICE, with but limited advantages for the acquisition of an education and contending with the embarrassments of poverty, commenced the stern battle of life, but with his vigorous intellect, his strong will, his unswerving honesty and integrity and his generous heart, he fought the battle bravely and successfully. And while he secured a competency as to fortune, he also secured that which was of far more value, the esteem and confidence of all with whom he was brought in contact; and on many occasions he received the strongest evidence of the high estimation in which he was held by his fellow-citizens, by being intrusted by their suffrages with high and important public duties.

As a man, Mr. RICE was distinguished for a strong, comprehensive, and vigorous intellect, quickened and trained by a long and active participation in the stirring scenes of active business, in which he acquired a large fund of practical and varied information. In manners he was affable, social, courteous, and dignified; in conversation, entertaining and instructive; and in all the relations of life, generous and magnanimous.

As a Representative in this Hall, where you all knew him, I need say but little of my late colleague. In the discharge of his public duties, the first and paramount question with him was, what is right? and when he had settled that question, he firmly adhered to his convictions, permitting no considerations of policy or expediency to swerve him from the right. He was unremitting in his attention to the business and wants of his constituents, prompt in his attendance upon and indefatigable in the performance of his duties in committee, regular and constant in his attendance upon the sessions of the House, and ever devoted himself industriously and conscientiously to the discharge of his whole duty to his constituents and to the country. He did discharge his duties nobly, faithfully, and well, and filled to the full the Jeffersonian standard of qualifications for public service. He was immovably honest, he was thoroughly capable, and he was diligently faithful. In a word, I repeat, Mr. Speaker, what I have said, that in his private as well as in his public life he was eminently distinguished for his immovable, unyielding, unflinching honesty and integrity. He earned and was justly entitled to that highest reward of the faithful public officer, "Well done, good and faithful servant." "Peace to his ashes."

Address of Mr. Fort, of Illinois.

Mr. Speaker: It was painful duty on a former occasion to announce to this House that death had been among the delegation from Illinois and had stricken down Hon. John B. Rice, Representative from the first district; and it is with tender sadness that I break silence here to-day to record my humble tribute of respect to the memory of my departed colleague.

I had known him before, but had formed no intimate acquaintance with him until our service began here together at the opening of this Congress. Our acquaintance soon became very agreeable to me. I soon discovered in him noble qualities and boundless generosity; I soon found that he was not only approachable but genial. It seemed to me that his manner and his bearing were not merely acquired, but that they sprang from native politeness and were founded upon broad benevolence and good-will toward all mankind. About him I never discovered anything low or vulgar; but to me his conversation always appeared elevating and his purposes honorable. To him I was indebted for information to me valuable, and which I still cherish with his memory.

The influence of his society was refining, and his companionship profitable. He desired that all mankind should be free and happy. He would always rather please than affront. Nature as well as culture had endowed and formed and fitted him to entertain his fellows. His service here was not all his public life. With other theaters he was more familiar, where he merited and received the popular favor. He was a loved and cherished companion, and a dear and indulgent father. He blessed his home and his fireside. The blow that removed him thence crushed and stunned the family circle.

When first we met here he seemed the most robust of all the delegation from our State. His sturdy and rugged form appeared able to wrestle with the labors and exposures of life for many years to come, and little did we think that he would be the first of us from Illinois to fall.

In his service here he worked hard and incessantly, and it is more than probable that his close application to his public duties during the long session, and his deep anxiety that all matters with which his country was concerned should go well, so wore upon him and sapped away his strength as to cause his premature end.

He loved his country more than he loved himself. He was true to the party with which he acted. All his political action was governed by principle, born of sincere conviction of what to him seemed right. For his political adversary he had no words of abuse. To his opponents he accorded the same freedom of opinion he claimed for himself, and to them he was always temperate and respectful. Like his great political leader, of whom he was a devoted follower, he had "charity for all and malice toward none."

But, Mr. Speaker, it is with no vain hope that I could fitly pronounce his eulogy that I do speak. I can at best but recognize the solemnity of the hour.

Death has been busy with us here on this floor. To his dread call no dilatory motions avail. There is no postponement to another day. The hammer falls and the victim is down forever. One after another our fellows fall around us and we inquire one of another, who will be the next? But this no one can tell. One by one our comrades are called; and they depart at once for that other country, and we seem to hear their spirits say, "Be ye also ready."

It is fitting, Mr. Speaker, that we should thus pause and hush the hum of our busy sessions and recognize the presence of death, that stalks unseen among us and treads unheard upon this floor. Unbidden and unwelcome have been its visits.

We shall never see the portly, manly form of my colleague stride up and down these aisles again; we shall hear the silvery tones of his commanding voice no more. When he fell some of us were appointed to attend his remains to the tomb. We followed them to his home in Chicago, of which city he had long been a resident and had been its chief magistrate. There the citizens both prominent and humble, and there his friends and neighbors gathered sorrowfully around his bier to pay their last tribute—there to gaze for the last time upon that form once so full of life and action; but it was cold and motionless. His once familiar voice, which had so often swayed and moved them to applause, was silenced forever; his eye that had so often beamed upon them was rayless and closed. And as they gazed there started many a tear from eyes unused to weep. Sadly we bore his remains to the grave in Rose Hill Cemetery, near his resident city, and silently and softly we laid them down to sleep until the morning of the resurrection, and peace be to his ashes was our prayer.

Our colleague has gone, gone on to that other city over on that beautiful shore.

Hail, brother; hail and farewell.

The resolutions offered by Mr. WARD, of Illinois, were then adopted unanimously.

PROCEEDINGS IN THE SENATE.

ADDRESS OF MR. OGLESBY, OF ILLINOIS.

I ask for the reading of the House resolutions announcing the death of Hon. JOHN B. RICE, which I believe are on the table, having been received from the House a few minutes ago.

The Secretary read as follows:

IN THE HOUSE OF REPRESENTATIVES,
February 20, 1875.

Resolved, That this House has heard with deep regret of the death of Hon. JOHN B. RICE, late a member of this House from the State of Illinois.

Resolved, That as a testimony of respect to his memory the officers and members of this House will wear the usual badge of mourning for the space of thirty days.

Resolved, That a copy of these resolutions be transmitted by the Clerk to the family of the deceased.

Mr. PRESIDENT: The solemn duty of announcing in this body the death of our honorable colleague of the other House would have fallen naturally and more appropriately upon my colleague, the senior Senator from Illinois. A short time ago, however, he advised me that he would have to forego his purpose of addressing the Senate upon this occasion in consequence of severe and painful sickness. I regret that my colleague is deprived of the sad privilege of performing the solemn duty of addressing the Senate at this hour. He was more familiarly acquainted with the dead member. I, however, knew him long enough and well enough to honor and love him. There was something more in his death than a loss to his fam-

ily.   There was a loss in some sense to the whole country.   He had
acted upon two stages in life—upon that common stage to which we
were all dedicated and upon that other one which has done so much
to enlighten and elevate mankind.   He was fond of the drama.   He
had studied all the great dramatists of ancient and modern times.
He was fond of works of fiction, and loved to study the human
character as portrayed by the best authors who had written upon it.

He was born in the midst of slavery, at some little village in the
State of Maryland, in 1809, and learned the trade of his father, that
of a shoemaker.   For years, I think, he followed this obscure but
honorable calling.   A strange circumstance changed his career.
Possessed of an unusually sweet voice, that gave expression to the tender feelings of a sweet soul, he arrested the common ear as day by
day he was toiling at his quiet seat.   Upon one such occasion an artist
in music, passing by the door of his shop, stopped to listen.   He at
once called upon the stranger, and from that hour Mr. RICE's occu-
pation in life was changed.   For the future he was dedicated to the
theater.   He went through the whole course of theatrical education,
and became a manager of large establishments successively in Philadelphia, in Buffalo, in Milwaukee, and finally in Chicago.   He was the
companion of such men as Forrest, the elder Booth, and that incom-
parably superior American genius, Charlotte Cushman.   Some of
her earliest performances were star engagements under the management of Mr. JOHN B. RICE in Buffalo and in Chicago.

I will not stop to follow his career in detail.   In many respects it
is the career of all men.   He had his troubles, his misfortunes, his
delays, in marching forward through the race of life; but it is enough
to say that he became distinguished in his profession.   He was abso-
lutely honored and more than respected; he was loved by all admir-
ers of that art.   Finally he abandoned it in 1857 and retired, as he
supposed, to private life, upon an entire competency.

Mr. RICE had one son and five daughters.   The only son he had he gave to his country; a brilliant and promising young man, the pride of a fond mother and proud father. Under the solicitation and encouragement of that father, the son enlisted as a private in the late war, soon became a captain, and on the 19th day of September, 1863, fell in leading his company forward into the battle of Chickamauga.

Mr. RICE was an intense patriot. Born, it is true, in Maryland, and in his youth habituated to the southern cast and shade of politics, he had, strange as it may seem from his peculiar associations, separated a long way from the masses of the people, from the common thoughts of that locality, and imbibed the spirit of anti-slavery. He became an active worker in the republican party at its very origin, and though mingling most of the time with associates not of his mode of thinking politically, he yet adhered steadfastly to his political faith up to the very hour of his death.

In 1865 the people of Chicago, who had great respect for him, insisted upon his running for mayor of that city. He consented, and was elected by a very large majority as the union republican candidate, and served two years. The people of that city insisted that he should again serve them in that capacity. He consented, and the second time was elected over a very strong opponent by a decided majority. At the end of his second term, which was again two years, he was for the third time urged by the people of that city to run once more for the office of mayor; but he declined and insisted upon retiring to private life. He did substantially retire to private life; but in 1872 the republican party in the city of Chicago, in the district where my colleague resides, insisted upon honoring him with their nomination for Congress. He had not sought it; he did not desire it. He had but little taste for politics; his tastes were almost exclusively literary. He consented, and over a very formidable antagonist was elected by an overwhelming majority. He entered the other House of Congress a stranger to most of the people of his own State, intimately acquainted with but very few of the members; a modest and retiring man, with great personal courage, great purity of purpose, great kindness of heart, great fidelity to what he believed to be right. He took his stand upon the republican side, and said:

I will support my party and its principles when it and its principles are right; but if I shall ever come conscientiously to doubt that its policies are correct, I will not follow them. I come to the halls of legislation to represent my people, and my chiefest object and my great purpose shall be that right and only right shall prevail in legislation.

He took no active or leading part. He was very industrious and and very faithful to his constituents, discharged all the ordinary duties that fall upon members of either House of Congress cheerfully and faithfully; occasionally spoke, and when he did speak in that House was listened to. He was a gentleman of fine presence, of captivating and alluring voice, fine taste in the use of language, and eloquent in all respects as a public speaker.

He was no scholar, Mr. President, in the proper and high sense of that term. He was a scholar in perhaps the too common American sense. His education was based upon experience; it was the result of a long line of observation, purely and almost entirely practical. He knew nothing of the greater and deeper sciences; he had not gone down to the very bottom of education; he had not fathomed the deepest and purest sources of thought. He was not, in that sense, either a philosopher or a student; but he was a man of eminent practical learning, practical wisdom, and had happily blended in him those qualities that arrested the attention of the learned and the rich, the lowly and the poor. All classes met upon his plateau. He was happily adapted by nature to all the various phases and changes of society—one of those few men who are ever at home with the highest and purest, ever at home with the lowest and poorest. Such a character, Mr. President, is an enviable one.

Mr. RICE did not live long enough to leave a reputation behind him as a representative of the people. He began to fail in health, and in the hope of being restored traveled largely last summer. Finally he went to Norfolk, Virginia, and, although past the meridian of life, was apparently in the midst of his usefulness; still vigorous, and, but for the sudden attack which seized him, had the promise of many years. He fell, however, and has gone down to the earth. He has passed away from life. But there was enough in that life to arrest deliberation in this great body, to arrest deliberation in that other great body at the other end of the Capitol. A nation stops for an hour to pass a brief, poor eulogy upon his character. How many there are who pass away unthought of, unremembered, and unnoticed! It was his happy lot to have earned the love, the respect, and confidence of all women and men who knew him, and to have arrested public attention in the halls of national legislation.

Farewell to the memory of JOHN B. RICE! Farewell to all the good acts and graces of his life! I join with my associates here in dropping a tear to his worthy name.

I ask, Mr. President, the adoption of the resolutions which I send to the desk.

The Secretary read the resolutions, as follows:

Resolved, That the Senate has received with profound sensibility the announcement of the death of Hon. JOHN B. RICE, late a member of the House of Representatives from the State of Illinois.

Resolved, That the members of the Senate, from a sincere desire of showing every mark of respect to the memory of Mr. RICE, will wear the usual badge of mourning for the space of thirty days.

Resolved, That the sympathies of the members of the Senate be tendered to the family of Mr. RICE in their bereavement, and that the Secretary of the Senate transmit to them a copy of these resolutions.

Address of Mr. Logan, of Illinois.

I rise merely to say that I sincerely regret that the condition of my health is such as to prevent me, as the senior Senator from Illinois, paying a proper tribute of respect to the memory of my deceased colleague in the other House. Mr. Rice was my friend and neighbor, and it would have been a source of sad satisfaction to me to have done him the honor that his life and character deserve.

Mr. President, I second the resolutions offered by my colleague.

The resolutions were adopted unanimously.

MEMORIAL ADDRESSES

ON THE

LIFE AND CHARACTER

OF

ALVAH CROCKER,

(A REPRESENTATIVE FROM MASSACHUSETTS,)

DELIVERED IN THE

SENATE AND HOUSE OF REPRESENTATIVES,

FEBRUARY 20, 1875.

PUBLISHED BY ORDER OF CONGRESS.

FORTY-THIRD CONGRESS, SECOND SESSION.

1875.

ADDRESSES

ON THE

DEATH OF ALVAH CROCKER.

PROCEEDINGS IN THE HOUSE OF REPRESENTATIVES.

ADDRESS OF MR. DAWES, OF MASSACHUSETTS.

Mr. SPEAKER: I desire to interrupt the ordinary current of business in this House that the attention of its members may be directed for a few moments to an event full of admonition, and one which awaits us all. It becomes my painful duty to announce to the House the death of one of its members, Hon. ALVAH CROCKER, a Representative from the tenth congressional district of Massachusetts, who died at his home in Fitchburgh, in that State, after a brief illness, on Saturday, the 26th day of December last. He separated from his colleagues and associates here at the commencement of the holiday recess in unusual health and spirits, speaking frequently of a vigor and freedom from illness not enjoyed for many years. His journey northward to his home in the rigor of December brought upon him a severe cold and afterward congestion of the lungs, which confined him to his house on Friday and terminated fatally on Saturday evening. He sank rapidly in the last few hours of his illness, and passed quietly away at eleven o'clock in the hope of a glorious immortality.

Mr. CROCKER was born in Leominster, in our State, on the 14th day of October, 1801, and had therefore at the time of his death just entered the seventy-fourth year of his age. His parents were poor, and without the means of rendering him any assistance in preparation for after life, and hardly more than a maintenance from his earliest years, and he became a factory operative when only eight years of age. The first and almost the only fifty dollars expended on his education was earned by him in night-work in the factory at four cents an hour, and while it lasted he was a pupil at Groton Academy. Whatever he could earn in this way was devoted by him to fitting himself for a broad and practical usefulness in after life. In fact, almost his entire education was acquired in that broader field of practical life where necessity is the teacher and experience the guide.

In his early manhood he entered as a partner with others into a responsible business connection as a manufacturer of paper, in which pursuit he continued with marked and unbroken success till his death. Though largely and devotedly engaged in this the special calling of his life, he found time to undertake and carry out to successful results other enterprises, some of them of vast public concern, and all of them of great usefulness and influence in promoting the healthy and permanent growth of the community in which he lived, bringing to himself at the same time large returns and ultimately great wealth.

Embarking with characteristic zeal and energy in the earliest railroad enterprise in Northern Massachusetts, if not himself its projector, at a time when railroads were as yet an untested experiment, he lived to see that line traverse the entire State and connect its tide-waters with the Hudson and the western lakes by one of the most marvelous works of internal improvements in modern times, and all pushed to completion by an energy and forecast inspired by him more than by any other. Under the same influences his own town has grown from an unimportant village of a few hundred inhabitants to a flourishing and prosperous city of large and increasing wealth and importance in the Commonwealth. It to-day mourns the loss of a citizen constantly contributing by a ceaseless activity singularly well directed to its improvement and prosperity, to the comfort and character and growth of its people.

Nor were these characteristics of Mr. CROCKER's life confined in their results to the city of his residence, but were felt in stimulating the development of a great variety of industrial interests and the consequent increase of prosperity and wealth in other parts of the State. A beautiful manufacturing town has sprung up within a few years on the banks of the Connecticut, increasing rapidly in population and wealth, and destined soon to rank among our cities, which owes its very existence to the indomitable energy and tireless efforts of Mr. CROCKER.

The implicit confidence of his fellow-citizens in his spotless integrity as well as sound judgment and unusual forecast, called him most frequently to positions of very delicate trust and of great responsibility, which he held from his earliest manhood to the day of his death. His decease has made vacant positions in the board of direction of institutions and associations for purposes of business and public and private trusts as well as for objects of benevolent and religious work greater in number and importance than would be caused by the death of almost any other citizen of the Commonwealth.

Mr. CROCKER was three times a member of the house and twice a senator in the Massachusetts Legislature. On the 2d day of January, 1872, he was elected to the Forty-second Congress to fill a vacancy caused by the resignation of Governor Washburn. His election took place while he was absent from the country with Mrs. Crocker, whose failing health had taken him abroad many months previous to the existence of the vacancy. He had no knowledge of either nomination or election till his return after both had occurred. Mrs. Crocker's protracted sickness and death detained him for some time from his seat. He was re-elected to the Forty-third Congress by a large majority, but declined a re-election to the Forty-fourth.

Mr. CROCKER was in politics a whig, and after that party a republican. Bringing to the discharge of every political duty growing out of those relations the same enthusiastic zeal which characterized his every undertaking, he was nevertheless no partisan, and always followed his convictions rather than his party. He came into Congress late in life, and was not permitted to remain long enough in his work here to leave that personal and permanent impression upon the administrative policy or legislation of the country which experience often brings to the share of others. But he was not idle here. Indeed, he could not be idle anywhere. In the committee-room, as well as upon the floor of the House, and always in consultation, his practical knowledge and wise counsel were invaluable, while his genial disposition and flow of conversation made him a general favorite. It was truthfully said of him that "he went directly at a thing in Congress as he would in his own business affairs, and in an earnest, homely way they were little accustomed to witness."

Mr. CROCKER was a remarkable man in all the variety of pursuits in life into which his tireless spirit and iron will led him to embark. A larger measure of success and a more wide-spread influence and abiding impression were attendant upon his career in life than mark the path of most of his contemporaries. The tendency of his whole life-work was for good. He was a generous giver, and especially delighted in aiding young men of limited means. The needy never turned empty from his door. No portion of that vast concourse of people who crowded the funeral procession testified their bereavement more sincerely than the humble and dependent who had been recipients of his bounty. He was a religious man, and died in the faith of the Protestant Episcopal Church, of which he was an officer at the time of his death.

Mr. CROCKER had been married three times, and left two children and a widow stricken by this bereavement, yet sustained by that faith which assures them that their loss is his gain.

Mr. Speaker, the shafts are falling thick and fast among us. Massachusetts is called upon by this dispensation, for the third time during this Congress, to mourn the loss of one from the number of those she has commissioned for the public service in these Halls. And even now, before these ceremonies are concluded, a fourth is added to the list of her dead. The funeral procession has but just borne another of her delegation from the scenes of his labor here. Our Commonwealth is most sensible of how great is that loss. She bows her head in submission and testifies her grief at the tomb of her faithful public servants.

I offer the following resolutions:

Resolved, That this House has heard with deep regret the death of Hon. ALVAH CROCKER, late a member of this House from the State of Massachusetts.

Resolved, That as a testimony of respect to the memory of the deceased the officers and members of this House will wear the usual badge of mourning for the space of thirty days.

Resolved, That a copy of these resolutions be transmitted by the Clerk to the family of the deceased.

ADDRESS OF MR. BUTLER, OF MASSACHUSETTS.

Mr. SPEAKER: The most gracious boon conferred by a merciful Providence upon any man is that he may not know the hour or manner of his death. When it comes to him in the full vigor of activity, especially after long, long years of a well-spent life, as a relief from all sorrow and care, with a humble Christian hope of a future and better life to come, such a departure calls neither for tears nor mourning in his behalf whose life has been so blessed by its ending. Yet it is well to pause amid the contests of life, its struggles and business, to give thought to the conduct and example of the departed, to contemplate all that is beautiful and good in his character, and to pay some tribute to his virtues, and thus aid to keep green his memory.

By the death of ALVAH CROCKER, a member from Massachusetts in this House of Representatives, our Commonwealth has been called a second time to mourn for one of her chosen men; and while he had not, from long services in the councils of the nation, high attributes of eloquence and learning, attained that exalted place in the affection and reverence of his countrymen that was held by the great statesman of our State whose death has within a twelvemonth called for our deepest sorrow, yet in another and perhaps no less useful sphere Mr. CROCKER has so well performed his part in life, and has left for the contemplation and imitation of the youth of the country a career no less honorable, and in its results to mankind quite as practical and beneficent.

From humble life, without the advantages of that early training and cultivation which the universities may give, brought up by the rugged hand of poverty, he early distinguished himself as a thorough man of affairs, whose foresight in planning, whose skill and energy in executing many most important undertakings for the welfare of his fellow-citizens and the prosperity of his State, early gave him an enviable reputation in a community where all the faculties of mind were taxed to the utmost in the most active and complicated duties of life.

Mr. CROCKER's character and success in life were indeed the very outgrowth of the industrial pursuits of the people of Massachusetts. At an almost infantile age an operative in a manufacturing establishment, thence steadily rising step by step, overseer, superintendent, owner, acquitting himself so well in all that each step was but the round of the ladder by which he climbed from honorable penury to competence and the like honorable wealth.   Among the very first of the far-seeing men of his State, with business sagacity that never faltered, he foresaw the effect which the then young system of railroading must have upon the prosperity of his native State, and allied himself very early in one of the most considerable railroad enterprises by which Boston was ultimately to be connected with the western part of New England, the provinces, the Canadas, and the great lakes.   His sagacity and business qualities were at once recognized by his associates in the enterprise, so that he was early made president of the Fitchburgh Railroad, planned in the beginning to connect his native town and the town of his adoption with Boston, but afterward to be extended so as to become a portion of the railroad system that connects the tide-waters of Boston Harbor with the great lakes and the granaries of the West.

Mr. CROCKER early saw, almost as by intuition, what came to others only by slow teachings of experience, the impossibility of profitably and effectively carrying on very extensive mercantile traffic over railroads encumbered by curves and heavy gradients, and therefore nearly a quarter of a century ago became the ardent advocate and untiring promoter of the most splendid engineering achievement of the age, the opening of a railroad track through Hoosac Mountain by a tunnel sufficient for a double-track road of quite five miles in extent, of which work the State gave him charge as its commissioner, and which he lived only long enough to see completed.

While possessing qualities of the most positive character, yet his nature was so kindly, his disposition so courteous, his mind so fair, and his conscience so just, that he had fewer collisions in the many and diverse kinds of business in which he took most active part than fall to the lot of the most favored few.   With such attributes, sustained by the most sturdy and vigorous physical health, which enabled him to carry forward with the greatest vigor all that he undertook, it was not singular that he early commanded the attention of his fellow-citizens as one well fitted for public service, and was by them chosen to represent their interests in public affairs; so that nearly forty years ago he was elected the representative of what is now the city of Fitchburgh to the legislature of Massachusetts, which he filled during several terms, and was afterward later in life elected to the senate of the State for two successive periods; in all which service he gained an enviable distinction and influence, never failing to command the suffrages of his fellow-citizens where he was offered as a candidate for their votes; so that he was elected twice to his seat in this House in the Forty-second and Forty-third Congresses, in which last we now turn aside from public affairs to mourn his loss as a fellow-member but yesterday acting with us in the business of the hour.

An ardent, patriotic friend of the Union, on the breaking out of the war Mr. CROCKER took the most active and intense interest in all measures for the suppression of the rebellion. Too far advanced in years to take part in arms, he exerted himself to send forward troops, and while the war was waging he made a voyage to England, and spent very considerable time in impressing upon the manufacturers of England the condition of our country and the necessity that there should be a community of interest and thought and mutual fellowship between those classes in both countries that represent the industries of the people. When the war was over, not unmindful of those who had gone forth at his solicitation to battle for the country and laid down their lives in its service on the battle-field, he exerted himself with his accustomed power and vigor, contributing thereto largely of his own means to provide that the fallen heroes of his city should have one of the most elaborate and costly of the many monuments erected to the memory of those who fell in battle in that war, and fortunately lived long enough to see it completed, having made the address at its dedication but a few months before his decease.

ALVAH CROCKER died at the age of upward of seventy-three years, but was possessed of such a strong and powerful frame and constitution of body, that it seemed probable but for the accidental contracting of the disease from which he died, he might have seen many more years of useful service to his country and his kind.

Such is the faint outline of the record of a life not so brilliant indeed as some that flash their light across the age in which they live, but so useful, so practical, so devoted to everything that could aid, prosper, and foster all the best interests of the community in which he lived, that it is more than doubted whether any better model of a life well spent and duty well done can be held up for the closest imitation of those who may come after him.

The resolutions submitted by Mr. DAWES were then unanimously adopted.

PROCEEDINGS IN THE SENATE.

ADDRESS OF MR. WASHBURN, OF MASSACHUSETTS.

I rise to ask for the reading of the resolutions from the House of Representatives in regard to my late colleague, Hon. ALVAH CROCKER, which I believe are on the table.

The VICE-PRESIDENT. The resolutions will be read.

The Secretary read as follows:

IN THE HOUSE OF REPRESENTATIVES,

February 20, 1875.

Resolved, That this House has heard with deep regret of the death of Hon. ALVAH CROCKER, late a member of this House from the State of Massachusetts.

Resolved, That as a testimony of respect to the memory of the deceased, the officers and members of this House will wear the usual badge of mourning for the space of thirty days.

Resolved, That a copy of these resolutions be transmitted by the Clerk to the family of the deceased.

I have presented the resolutions which have been read with feelings of peculiar sadness. Never before has our State, never before has any State since the formation of the Government been called to mourn the loss of so large a percentage of its delegation during a given Congress. Four during the term, three in the past year, nearly one-third of our delegation have fallen in the ranks. Death came so sudden and unexpected upon each one that their most intimate friends hardly realized that they had withdrawn from their daily official labors. Surely the reaper has thrust his sickle into our ranks with no sparing hand.

During the last session Mr. CROCKER being confined to his room for a long time by severe sickness, none of us would have been surprised at the news of his death at any moment. But soon after his return home in the summer he began to improve and recovered his usual strength and vigor, so that when he returned to his official duties at the commencement of the present session he had the appearance of a strong, healthy man. A few days previous to our late recess he left for home to spend the holidays with the members of his family and near relatives of his own house. When he reached home he had a slight cold, but not sufficient to cause the least alarm. He applied himself from day to day to the inspection of his business affairs till Christmas, when he found himself too unwell to participate in the festivities of the day. It was not, however, until Saturday evening that he felt the necessity of medical attendance. His family physician was summoned, and upon examination pronounced the disease to be congestion of the lungs, not of such a nature, however, as to cause alarm. But he gradually failed during the day, and, finally, at eleven o'clock in the evening, died while sitting in his chair. Thus he passed over the river before many beyond his own family circle knew of his sickness.

Mr. CROCKER was born in Leominster, Mass., October 14, 1801, and consequently was seventy-three years of age at the time of his death. His father, a hard-working, energetic man, was a paper manufacturer. He placed his son Alvah in the mill to learn the trade when but eight years of age. The boy was anxious to secure for himself better educational advantages than could be obtained at that time in our public schools. By practicing the most rigid economy he was enabled to acquire an academical education.

When twenty-two years of age he moved to the neighboring town of Fitchburgh, and commenced the manufacture of paper for himself. Beginning with nothing but an inheritance of poverty and toil, he struggled along against untold difficulties and with varied success. With means so very limited he was obliged to commence in a small way, but gradually extended his business as he was able until he became the important proprietor of six or eight large establishments, and one of the most extensive and most successful paper manufacturers in the country.

But his time and energies were by nó means confined to the prosecution of his own business. He was a man of liberal views and large public spirit; he took special interest in the prosperity and growth of the town in which he lived. He did more than any other inhabitant to develop its resources; he devoted not only his time but most liberally his means to this end. From a small town of some two thousand inhabitants when he commenced business it has grown to be one of the most beautiful, thrifty cities in the State, with a population of over fifteen thousand. The variety of its industries, the busy hum of its machinery, its railroad facilities quickening into renewed intensity the exchanges of business and the intercourse of men, all combine to make it one of the most attractive municipalities in the State. Mr. CROCKER desired to develop and utilize every waterfall in the town. To this end he secured new and unexpected means of transportation to, and communication with, every section of the State. Not that his vision was narrowed and circumscribed within the limits of his own town.

When the system of railroads had hardly been commenced, when but few miles had been built in the country, when most business men refused to risk their capital in such visionary enterprises, Mr. CROCKER conceived the idea of constructing a railroad from his town to Boston, in order that the northern part of the State might have free and easy access to the seaboard. He labored long and earnestly to secure a charter for this road. He met with considerable opposition uot only from many of the most influential men in the eastern part of the State, but also from those who resided along the line of the route. It was thought that the scheme would end in utter failure.

region which yesterday was a desolate, barren waste has to-day become a beautiful, flourishing town with its thousands of inhabitants. The beautiful churches, school-houses, and public and private structures of every variety attract the attention and call forth the admiration of the beholder. A national bank of discount and a savings institution each bear his name, and he was the president of each. Turner's Falls stands to-day with its wonderful improvements as a monument to the energy and foresight of Mr. CROCKER.

Mr. CROCKER served three terms in the lower and two in the upper house of the Massachusetts legislature with credit to himself and honor to his constituents. In 1871 he visited Europe on account of the sickness of his wife, and during his absence was elected to the Forty-second Congress, to fill the vacancy caused by my resignation. He was re-elected to the Forty-third Congress by 14,919 votes against 4,588 for the democratic candidate. He declined to be a candidate at the last election. When he entered upon his duties here he was over seventy years of age, and much of the time his health was so impaired that it was with difficulty that he attended to his official duties. In public as in private life he was strictly honest. He discharged all his duties in a most conscientious manner. No jobbery or corruption was ever traced to his door; but his entire record stands above suspicion.

Of his private life, of his genial and liberal hospitality, of the strength and warmth of his friendship, there is no time or need of reference on this occasion. Beyond the immediate circle of his friends, he will be specially mourned by the large company of his business associates among whom the greater part of his daily life has been passed, by the thousands of employés who were more or less dependent on him for their daily sustenance, and by that untold number who have been the recipients for many long years of his charities.

Mr. CROCKER was not without his faults. Like most men he

made his mistakes and had his weaknesses. But on such an occasion as this we may well forget these. If we estimate his worth by what he has accomplished for the community in which he lived, for the section of the State in which he resided, few men will bear comparison with him. May it be ours to gather up and cherish the memory of his many virtues.

Mr. President, I send to the desk resolutions which I offer for the consideration of the Senate.

The VICE-PRESIDENT. The resolutions will be read.

The Secretary read as follows:

Resolved, That the Senate has received with deep sensibility the announcement of the death of Hon. ALVAH CROCKER, late a member of the House of Representatives from the State of Massachusetts.

Resolved, That as a mark of respect for the memory of Mr. CROCKER, the members of the Senate will wear the usual badge of mourning for thirty days.

Resolved, That a copy of these resolutions be transmitted by the Secretary of the Senate to the family of the deceased.

ADDRESS OF MR. WADLEIGH, OF NEW HAMPSHIRE.

Mr. PRESIDENT: A residence of some years near the home of ALVAH CROCKER and a knowledge of his reputation there lead me to pay a brief tribute to his memory.

His reputation was not won in political warfare nor in public life. Five years in the Massachusetts legislature and two in the national House of Representatives after the age of three-score and ten were not sufficient for that. Yet he always manifested good sense, sincerity, praiseworthy fidelity to the interests of his constituents, and enlarged patriotism.

But his reputation was won in the course of a long and successful business career. Beginning life in obscurity and poverty, at the early age of eight years he was a factory operative. But his energy and ability conquered adverse circumstances. He secured an education which furnished a foundation for business success, and achieved a large fortune. That fortune was not used mainly for his personal advantage; it was used to forward and complete enterprises which have largely contributed to the growth and prosperity of Northern Massachusetts. The people whose welfare he had promoted manifested their respect for him by sending him to represent them in Congress when at the advanced age of seventy-one years by an overwhelming majority.

What can be said of him in these Halls will do comparatively little to perpetuate his memory. He has a nobler and more enduring monument than speech can rear. In Worcester County, upon the rocky banks of a flashing river hurrying swiftly to the sea, stands one of the most beautiful and thriving cities of New England, which within a few years has been created and which owes very of much what it is to the business ability and public spirit of ALVAH CROCKER. Till that city perishes will his memory be preserved as one of its founders.

The resolutions were adopted unanimously.

MEMORIAL ADDRESSES

ON THE

LIFE AND CHARACTER

OF

SAM'L F. HERSEY,

(A REPRESENTATIVE FROM MAINE,)

DELIVERED IN THE

SENATE AND HOUSE OF REPRESENTATIVES,

FEBRUARY 20, 1875.

PUBLISHED BY ORDER OF CONGRESS.

FORTY-THIRD CONGRESS, SECOND SESSION.

1875.

ADDRESSES

ON THE

DEATH OF SAM'L F. HERSEY,

PROCEEDINGS IN THE HOUSE OF REPRESENTATIVES.

ADDRESS OF MR. HALE, OF MAINE.

Mr. SPEAKER: We are but five in all in this House from the State of Maine when all are present, and one of our number has been taken away by death. Hon. SAMUEL FREEMAN HERSEY, who represented the fourth district of Maine in this Congress, died at his home in Bangor on the 3d day of this month. The fatal disease that at last ended in death fastened upon him many months ago and broke down the physical strength which had been marked in his previous life. It interfered seriously with his duties in the last session of this Congress, driving him from the Capitol in the late winter months after he had resolutely fought its approaches, turned his home during the summer and fall into a house of sickness, and inexorably forbade any attempt to share in the labors and duties of the present session. The resolute will of my late colleague and friend was so noticeable a feature in his character that I shall be well borne out by those who knew him best in saying that nothing less than the painful disease under which he suffered could have kept him away from the post to which a trusting people had called him. As I remember him and recall an acquaintance of many years, there arises before me no instance when he shrank from a duty laid upon him.

General HERSEY was born in Sumner, in the county of Oxford, and State of Maine, on the 22d of April, 1812. He came from revolutionary stock, his maternal grandfather having been an officer in the war for Independence; and he was reared in that best school for early boyhood which the New England fireside, hillside, and school-house furnish. When at the age of twenty-one he entered upon mercantile business for himself, he had secured the good education that the district school and the county academy afforded, and was well fitted to enter into the conflict of active life. In business he almost always prospered, increasing his ventures and his gains from year to year, and, latterly, extending his operations into Minnesota, Wisconsin, and other Northwestern States. He was prompt and energetic in affairs; honest and conscientious in his dealings; and as his fortune increased gave liberally of his store.

He was always trusted by the people among whom he lived, representing the town of Milford in the lower house of the Maine legislature in 1842; the city of Bangor, to which he afterward removed, in one branch or the other of the State legislature in 1857, 1865, 1867, and 1869; besides serving for some years as a member of the executive council. After filling other important State offices, he was first elected to this House in September, 1872, and was re-elected in 1874. From participation in what promised to be the stirring scenes of the Forty-fourth Congress, he has been cut off. Had he lived, his position must always have been clearly defined. His was never a halting or doubtful course. His religious and political beliefs were a part of his life; and he accepted the consequences of those beliefs boldly.

This positiveness of character led him not to fear antagonism; but his kindness of heart raised up friends and prevented life-long enmities.

Mr. Speaker, our deceased colleague will be greatly missed in our own State, where he has been for years a prominent citizen; to his neighbors and friends the loss will come nearer; to his family it can never be repaired.   On this floor those who knew him during the brief weeks that he was in attendance know that this House has lost an honest, useful member.

But awful as is the coming of death, and sobering as must be its contemplation, the way along which a human life is sometimes led to it is so beset with suffering and agony that to our limited vision the final summons must then seem more like a relief than a doom.

General HERSEY'S disease was severe and protracted.   It never broke down his mind or his spirit, but it wasted his body and racked him with pain such as few men fortunately are ever called to endure. It was incurable; and at last he sank under it.   But he died in his own house, with his wife and children about him, and loving hands smoothed his winter shroud.   Thinking of how vexed had been his last days and how peaceful was his death, who will not ask with Spenser—

> Is not short pain well borne that brings long ease
>   And lays the soul to rest in quiet grave?
> Sleep after toil, port after stormy seas,
> Peace after war, death after life doth sometimes greatly please.

Mr. Speaker, I move the following resolutions:

Resolved, That this House has heard with deep regret the death of Hon. SAMUEL F. HERSEY, a member of this House from the State of Maine.

Resolved, That as a testimonial of respect to the memory of the deceased, the officers and members of this House will wear the usual badge of mourning for the space of thirty days.

Resolved, That a copy of these resolutions be transmitted by the Clerk to the family of the deceased.

ADDRESS OF MR. FRYE, OF MAINE.

The ordinary labors of this legislative hall are suspended, its confusion hushed, and a new spirit holds supremacy here now.   A remarkable event induces silence and solemnity, admonishing us that—

> Art is long and time is fleeting,
>   And our hearts, though stout and brave,
> Still like muffled drums are beating
> Funeral marches to the grave—

admonishes us that life is uncertain and death is certain; admonishes us that what we have to do we ought to do quickly and well.

Sir, death is making a terrible havoc in our ranks   Within less than one year six members of the New England delegation in Congress have died, each one of whom in his chosen business or walk in life was a pre-eminently successful man.   Statesmanship, law, commerce, and manufactures have made monumental contributions to the city of the dead.   To-day the death of three of them has been announced on this floor; two, men full of years and full of honors, each of whom had reached nearly if not quite that allotment to man's life of three score years and ten; each of them like a ripe shock of corn gathered to his fathers, leaving a legacy behind him of a well-rounded and perfect life.

Our colleague, General HERSEY, was cut down in the very prime and vigor of life.   To the casual observer his work, though well done, was only half done; his life a partial failure, his battle not fought out, and the broken shaft would be a fitting monument to his memory, the emblem of life incomplete.   But to us who knew him well and for years have known him well he had finished his fight and won the victory; he had run the race and reached the goal.   Were we to build his monument, its base would be broad, strong, deep laid, where no frost could heave and no tempest move; and its shaft should be beautiful, white, perfect.

To his business career General HERSEY brought earnestness of purpose, strict integrity, economy, habits of industry, and an indomitable will. His hope was so bright and buoyant that no defeat ever made him despondent; his courage was so strong and sure that no lion in his path ever turned him aside; his integrity so strict and steadfast that no shadow of suspicion ever darkened his fair name. I remember, when he with others was surety on a defaulting State treasurer's bonds, he interposed no legal technicality, not even an equitable defense, but promptly paid every dollar not only that the law could demand, but all a quickened and sensitive conscience could suggest. Such was his sagacity that his plans never miscarried.

The city he lived in and his State poured wealth into his coffers; and, as my colleague has well said, the States of the great West, too, were compelled to contribute, until when he died he was one of the wealthiest, if not the wealthiest, man in Maine. Then, sir, as a business man stainless, owing no man, neither defrauding nor dealing hardly with any man; indulging in no rash and reckless speculations; prosperous, successful in every endeavor; rich beyond his most ardent hopes—do I not say well, his life was complete?

But, sir, could I say nothing more than this it would seem to me but the cold praise exacted by strict justice. My heart would give no response; my affection pay no tribute. A man's life lived for self alone is a failure. General HERSEY lived another, a higher, a purer, a nobler life than this of amassing wealth. The stream which turns the wheel of the mill and drives the spindle and the loom does its duty; but never this alone. All along its course, from its source to its mouth, it continually makes green the grass, waters the flowers, gives life to the tree. So General HERSEY all through his long, active, business career never for one moment when overtaking and passing by his less fortunate fellow-man forgot him, but stretched out to him a helping hand, gave him words of good cheer.

And I know of many a man to-day in my own State and some here, living now in comfort, who owe all that they have to his kind words and liberal deeds.

> For his bounty
> There was no winter in't; an autumn 't was,
> That grew the more by reaping.

In social life General HERSEY was the gayest among the gay, his presence always joyfully received, and his absence always felt with grief. To the poor, the feeble, and the dependent his face always brought with it healing, strength, and hope. His hearty, cheerful manner was like the sunbeam breaking through the prison-bars, making for the whiles the gloom of the cell brightness.

The cause of education lost one of its best and most beneficent friends when he died. Institutions of learning in my own State and in others to-day mourn for the loss of a liberal, bountiful benefactor. In politics he was always welcome to the party whose policy he espoused, for he was one of the most zealous, earnest men I ever saw, giving new strength and courage to his party.

His people loved him; and there never was an office in their gift he could not command; yet his modesty led him to accept but few. The devotion of his constituents was well illustrated in the fact, as my colleague has stated, that here in this House for this term of Congress he has been nearly the whole time unable to perform any of the ordinary duties of a member, yet before the last election, though most understood, or feared at least, that he was upon his dying bed, he was renominated by acclamation and re-elected by an increased majority.

It may be and it may seem to many gentlemen a little thing, but I cannot help mentioning it in filling out this life of my colleague, that if you walked with him through the streets of his native city you would see little children greeting him and he them all along your way.

Sir, I tell you the man who loves children and whom children love is not and cannot be a bad man. The children of his Sunday-school, to whom he had again and again given words of wisdom and counsel, met the other day in his native city and passed resolutions indicative of sorrows at their irreparable loss.

The church mourns General HERSEY as one of its pillars broken. His memory will be fresh and green always. He was no sectarian; he was no bigot; but he loved with his whole heart the church of his choice. I remember Webster once said " religion is a necessary and indispensable element in any great human character." My late colleague was a religious man. His religion can be summed up in two commandments, "To love God and to love one's neighbor." We who knew him knew that he could pray ; for

> He prayeth best who loveth best
> All things both great and small;
> For the dear God who loveth us,
> He made and loveth all.

Sir, did I not say well, then, that his life was well rounded, and perfect, too ?

Our sympathies, sir, go out to his bereaved family. They have suffered a loss for which now they can see no compensation whatever. To the widow and to the fatherless children we can only say, "Death ·is the crown of such a life."

ADDRESS OF MR. DUNNELL, OF MINNESOTA.

· Mr. SPEAKER : In the winter of 1854, at Augusta, the capital of Maine, I formed the acquaintance of the late SAMUEL F. HERSEY. He was at that time in the full strength of middle life, and was among the foremost of the leading business men of Eastern Maine.

That rank he held till continued ill-health, commencing soon after his election to this Congress, compelled his retirement.

Mr. HERSEY had his birth at Sumner, in the county of Oxford, in 1812. At his majority, or soon after, he sought his home and theater of labor in the city of Bangor, the then central point of the large lumbering interests of Maine. At this period in the history of the State, his adopted home was especially noted for the enterprise and ability of its professional and business men. Its prosperity and prom- ise had drawn to it from the neighboring counties, and indeed from the neighboring States, not a few men who have since then honored the State in every department of life. This comparatively new city at that time welcomed every bold comer. Mr. HERSEY, at the very start of his business life, was as bold in purpose as in form were the hills of his native county. He entered the race to reach the goal. Success in honorable business was the end he sought. That end he attained by wise foresight, just means, unflagging endeavor, and unimpeachable character.

His large acquisitions, the manner, time, and place of his invest- ments, attest a superior order of judgment. The steady increase in the rewards to his industry indicates the possession of a mind which could and did grasp all the conditions of success. His eminent prosperity was not a result of chance. He had it because he deserved it; because his plans and courses of action by an inevitable law gave it to him.

As time passed and his means increased, his operations were largely diversified. He was a merchant, banker, and lumberman. He invested in timber-lands, both East and West, in mining, insurance, banking, and railroads. Maine has not alone witnessed his achieve- ments. In 1854 he commenced the purchase of timber-lands in Minnesota and Wisconsin, and with others erected a mill for the manufacture of lumber at Stillwater, in the State of Minnesota. Since that time he has had large interests at that point and elsewhere in the State. His money has aided in the construction of at least two of the railroads in our State.   He owned at the time of his death not less than seventy-five thousand acres of timber-lands in Minnesota and Wisconsin, and no inconsiderable amount in Michigan and Maine.

Minnesota, therefore, Mr. Speaker, unites with Maine in expressions of profound sorrow at the death of a citizen so eminently deserving the honors conferred upon him in his native State and the respect paid him wherever known.   As sincere mourners dwell on the banks of the Saint Croix and of the Mississippi as of the Penobscot.   So large were his investments in the State and so early did he participate in her development that we almost deemed him an addition to our own delegation to this House.   While he had his home in the East, he was deeply in love with the West.   He appreciated the extent and character of her needs and her capacities.   He fully realized her immense possibilities, and was ready to favor measures which, to the more conservative, seemed little less than visionary.

Mr. HERSEY was thrice married.   Four sons were the fruit of the second marriage.   Two of these sons are residents of Maine and two of Minnesota.

Prior to 1854 the deceased was a member of the democratic party. Up to that year he followed the fortunes of this party with the same enthusiasm and devotion with which he afterward, and till his death, sustained those of the republican.   He was five times a member of the Maine house of representatives and twice a member of the executive council.   In addition to other honors, he was elected to this and the Forty-fourth Congress.   In politics, he was sincere and earnest.   His convictions found expression in bold and straight-forward action.   His position on pending questions was never left to conjecture.   He was sufficiently radical to be secure against the temptations of a timid and therefore dangerous conservatism.   His patriotism was too ardent to lend its ear to the voice of mere policy.   He was a most valuable member of the republican party, for he was in it from conviction and was unswerving and unceasing in labor and counsel to keep alive that aggressive spirit which leads to party achievement. He did not falter, though others fell behind.

> Among innumerable false, unmoved,
> Unshaken, unseduced, unterrified,
> His loyalty he kept, his love, his zeal;
> Nor number, or example with him wrought,
> To swerve from truth or change his constant mind,
> Though single.

Mr. HERSEY was not well known to the members of this House. He came here a sick man and therefore was not himself. His sickness affected his mind and spirit as well as body. When in health his mind was intensely active and his spirits always buoyant. He was happy in every place and amid all labors; he was free and genial; his manners made him friends, and his open kindness gave him influence.

His donations to institutions of learning and to churches were very considerable. Many a locality will long cherish his memory. His accumulations of wealth did not make him deaf to the calls of the poor or forgetful of the teachings of religion. Our friend died at home. Death approached him in slow, yet certain steps. He saw the enemy at a distance and watched his advance. He had months in which to review life's work and bring to his lips, "Thy will be done." His faith in the world's Redeemer took away every fear of the grave. He had wrought life's work with a fervent heart; his duties had been well performed and his days well spent.

> O, what a glory doth this world put on
> For him who, with fervent heart, goes forth
> Under the bright and glorious sky, and looks
> On duties well performed, and days well spent!
> For him the wind, ay, and the yellow leaves,
> Shall have a voice and give him eloquent teachings.
> He shall so hear the solemn hymn, that Death
> Has lifted up for all, that he shall go
> To his long resting-place without a tear.

The question was taken on the resolutions, and they were unanimously agreed to.

PROCEEDINGS IN THE SENATE.

A message from the House of Representatives, by Mr. McPherson, its Clerk, communicated to the Senate intelligence of the death of Hon. SAMUEL F. HERSEY, late a member of the House of Representatives from the State of Maine, and transmitted the resolutions of the House thereon.

ADDRESS OF MR. HAMLIN, OF MAINE.

I rise for the purpose of asking the Senate to consider the resolutions just communicated from the House of Representatives.

The VICE-PRESIDENT. The resolutions will be read.

The Secretary read the resolutions of the House of Representatives, as follows:

Resolved, That this House has heard with deep regret of the death of Hon. SAMUEL F. HERSEY, late a member of this House from the State of Maine.

Resolved, That as a testimony of respect for the memory of the deceased, the officers and members of this House will wear the usual badge of mourning for the space of thirty days.

Resolved, That a copy of these resolutions be transmitted by the Clerk to the family of the deceased.

Mr. PRESIDENT: The resolutions which have just been read, informing the Senate of the decease of my colleague in the House, furnish another admonition to us all of the frailty of human existence. Another seat has been made vacant in the Halls of Congress. Its warning may, as it should, subserve a useful purpose. The event, though not unexpected, brings to myself a sorrow that I cannot express. The deceased was my friend. In all the relations and vicissitudes of life, in all its changing scenes, from youth to manhood, from manhood to mature age, and for more than half the period of life allotted to man, we were knit together in an unceasing and unbroken friendship. He was a friend who could "bear a friend's infirmities." How impressively am I reminded, as it becomes my sad duty to pay an earnest and truthful tribute to his memory and his worth, that under the decrees of an inscrutable Providence he might well have been spared to perform a like service to mine.

General HERSEY came to this city at the commencement of the present Congress to discharge the duties which had been imposed upon him by a generous and confiding constituency. He was then in feeble health; but having been possessed of great physical power, it was the hope and belief of himself and friends that a more genial climate than his home afforded would restore him to health. In that hope all have been disappointed. Failing health, however, compelled him, much against his will, to withdraw from active participation in his official duties, and to seek the best medical advice that could be afforded in a neighboring city. From thence he repaired to his own home in an apparently improved and improving condition, giving to his friends a renewed hope of his permanent recovery. This hope was strengthened by his own faith, which impressed itself upon all around him, giving assurance even to the despondent. Indeed, his own belief in his final and full recovery was marvelous, and he held it with unsubdued courage to the last. He endured his sufferings and sickness with remarkable fortitude and cheerfulness. From their commencement to their close he murmured not. When absent from home, all that kindness and attention could do to alleviate his condition was done. But to me, and I may say to all my colleagues, it is a matter of consolation to know that friends, and home, and wife, and children all contributed to cheer and mitigate his pain and sufferings in the last days and hours of his life. There is no place to those who suffer like home; no hand to minister, no voice to cheer, like that of an affectionate wife. Stricken with a disease which baffled all medical skill and defied the affectionate care of wife and friends, on the 3d of the present month, without a struggle, his spirit took its flight to "the better land;" and all of him that was mortal reposes to-day in the soil of his native State.

Virtue alone has majesty in death.

General HERSEY was a native of the State of Maine, to the manor born. He was born in the town of Sumner, county of Oxford, in the month of April, 1812. At his decease he was nearly sixty-three years of age. His early years, like those of most young men of that time, were devoted to agricultural pursuits upon his father's farm, where those habits of industry were established which marked his future life and to which he was indebted for his great success. He was studious in his habits, and availed himself of the common school and academy, in which he acquired a good, substantial English education. Ambitious for a broader field than the farm afforded, and at a time near his majority, he entered the counting-room to prepare and fit himself for mercantile and business pursuits, in which he subsequently became distinguished. Several years of his life were devoted to merchandising; and afterward extending his business to the manufacture and sale of lumber in his own and some of the North-western States, he became one of the most extensive and successful lumbermen of the country.

He was a republican in principle, understanding fully the wants of the country and the duties of the hour. He was no bigot, but conceded to others the rights of opinion which he so firmly maintained for himself. From the formation of the republican party until the time of his death he gave to its support a mature judgment and an energy of purpose and personal efforts which made him a power in that organization. He loved his whole country, and through all the dark and trying hours of the war, when it trembled in the balance, he contributed to it his earnest and efficient support, and his eldest son did gallant service in the Army.

He has been prominent in the administration of the affairs of the State; and was an honor to his State, as his State had honored him.

In the years 1842, 1857, and 1865 he was a member of the house of representatives of the State; and in the years 1867 and 1869 he served in the State senate. In 1852 and 1853 he was a member of the executive council. In 1870 he was induced by his friends to be a candidate for the republican nomination for governor, and came witin a very few votes of receiving the nomination. In 1872 he was nominated for Congress in the fourth district, and elected by over five thousand majority; and was re-elected to the Forty-fourth Congress at the annual election in September last. Besides these he held other important political and public trusts. The duties devolved upon him in all these varied positions were discharged with ability, fidelity, and integrity. That speaks his own best eulogy.

General HERSEY was an honest man—"God's noblest work." He was a man of unsullied and spotless integrity; peerless in his purity. In the counting-room or on the public mart his word was the equivalent of his bond. He was a man of public enterprise, and entered with zeal into every measure which would elevate the character of his State or city or promote the welfare of the people, however humble. He was benevolent and charitable, as the poor who were the recipients of his bounty can attest. While his contributions to all of our charitable institutions were of a generous character, many were the charities he bestowed unseen and unknown by the public.

He was an earnest friend of the cause of education; has contributed liberally to institutions of learning, and has left large bequests for its future aid and support. He was an earnest worker in the church of which he was a member. How much he contributed, how invaluable were his services, how constant he was in the discharge of all his varied duties, the church itself can best know. But that his services were invaluable, that his duties were well performed, and that his contributions were of the most liberal character, even those not closely associated with him are well informed. How he will be missed and mourned within that circle!

He was a Christian gentleman, and his daily life adorned his profession. He was best loved by those who knew him best. His loss will be sincerely felt and mourned by all classes of the community in which he lived, from the highest to the most humble. I mourn the loss of a sincere friend. The State is bereft of one of her distinguished sons; his constituents are deprived of the valuable and efficient services of an able Representative. In the home circle, as husband and father, he was genial, kind, and affectionate. He strove to make and did make home what it should be—the most endearing spot on earth. A widowed wife and children weep in a home made desolate for the irreparable loss of a kind husband and an affectionate father; but into that mourning circle it is not my province to enter. Time, "with healing in its wings," will assuage their grief, and their reliance must be on "Him who doeth all things well."

The House has paid a tribute to his worth and have manifested their appreciation of the man in their resolutions which have been communicated to the Senate. I ask the Senate to join with the House in an expression of respect for the deceased and of sympathy for the surviving relatives by adopting the resolutions which I now send to the Chair.

The Secretary read the resolutions, as follows:

Resolved, That the Senate receives with sincere regret the announce-

ment of the death of Hon. SAMUEL F. HERSEY, late a member of
the House of Representatives from the State of Maine, and tenders
to the relatives of the deceased the assurance of their sympathy with
them under the bereavement they have been called to sustain.

Resolved, That the Secretary of the Senate be directed to transmit
to the family of Mr. HERSEY a certified copy of the foregoing reso-
lution.

ADDRESS OF MR. MORRILL, OF MAINE.

Mr. PRESIDENT: The bereavement which arrests the proceedings
of the Senate touches so many hearts with tenderest sorrow in the
State that honors me with its confidence, and withal sunders ties of
friendly and official relations, that I trust to be indulged in adding
a few words to what has already been so feelingly and appropriately
said.

The claims of Mr. HERSEY upon our respect spring from an unsullied character, from his personal virtues and public services. By the
inherent energies and fidelity of his nature, unaided by adventitious
supports, he had acquired affluence in private affairs, had often been
associated in the councils of his State, and had at length entered
those of the nation, alas! unhappily, soon to fall under the heavy
hand of disease, which ere long was to remove him hence.

His was an active and useful life in the departments of practical
duty and endeavor, whereby society is advanced through a community of interests, the general welfare, the highest good of the greatest number.

He was ever the sagacious, upright, eminently successful man of
business, of generous impulses, of a truly catholic spirit, charitable,
liberal, and humane, whose daily life was without reproach, and was
an example to all. He has sprung from among the people in the
common walks of life, was by the simplicity of his tastes, the habits
formed in pursuits intimately connected with their interests, and by

his truly democratic intentions always in deepest sympathy with them, and was therefore fitly and not infrequently their trusted Representative.

The memory of Mr. HERSEY will be cherished by the people of Maine as among the public men who had rendered valuable public service in its councils, who in private life was faithful to every duty, to the obligations of friendship, and the claims of good neighborship.

Mr. President, I second the resolutions offered by my colleague.

The resolutions were adopted unanimously.

MEMORIAL ADDRESSES

ON THE

LIFE AND CHARACTER

OF

SAMUEL HOOPER,

(A REPRESENTATIVE FROM MASSACHUSETTS,)

DELIVERED IN THE

SENATE AND HOUSE OF REPRESENTATIVES,

FEBRUARY 20, 1875.

PUBLISHED BY ORDER OF CONGRESS.

FORTY-THIRD CONGRESS, SECOND SESSION.

1875.

ADDRESSES

DEATH OF SAMUEL HOOPER.

PROCEEDINGS IN THE HOUSE OF REPRESENTATIVES.

ADDRESS OF MR. E. R. HOAR, OF MASSACHUSETTS.

In the death of SAMUEL HOOPER, the last of our associates who has been summoned from the scenes of his earthly labors, we have been called to part with a member of this body one of the oldest of our number, one of the longest in continuous service, and one of the most generally esteemed and respected.

He was born in Marblehead, on the 3d of February, 1808. His father and grandfather were merchants, and he came of that sturdy race of men who for two centuries have peopled the shores of Massachusetts Bay, making it the nursery of seamen, the home of shipmasters, and the birthplace of so large a proportion of those whose enterprise and sagacity have whitened every sea with the sails of American commerce; the men of courage, endurance, clear heads, and large hearts, who have gathered wealth in every field of commercial adventure to pour it out freely in response to any call of patriotism, of public spirit, of religion, education, learning, or public or private charity.

His father was the president of .the old Marblehead Bank, one of the solid moneyed institutions of an elder generation. He was thus by birth and training fitted for the employment to which most of his life was devoted, that of a merchant and financier, in which he achieved such eminent distinction and success. In his early life he went as supercargo in his father's vessels to Cuba and Russia and Spain. He married a daughter of William Sturgis, and thereupon became a partner in the house of Bryant & Sturgis, and engaged in the trade with China and the northwest coast. On the dissolution of that firm he became a partner of William Appleton, his predecessor in Congress, continuing the large and varied business of the house, after the death of Mr. Appleton, under the name of Samuel Hooper & Co. By inheritance and marriage he had a considerable property, which he increased to the dimensions of a large fortune. His wife, two daughters, and several grandchildren survive him, but he had borne the heavy sorrow of the loss of his only son.

His public life consisted of three years' service in the Massachusetts house of representatives, a single term in the State senate, and the fourteen years in which he has represented one of the Boston districts in Congress.

Mr. HOOPER first attracted notice in connection with public affairs by the vigor with which, when a member of the whig party, he addressed himself to the defense of the doctrine of hard money and the stringent regulation of whatever substitute therefor might be devised, which brought him for a time somewhat in affiliation with the democrats. He became early a member of the republican party, and during his whole term of service in Congress represented that party upon this floor.

To most of those of us who are members of Congress for the first time Mr. HOOPER's position and strength in this House are very much matters of tradition. But with his large experience, with his native shrewdness, with his clearness of mind and uprightness of purpose, he brought to the public service here when he first entered upon it qualities of conspicuous value.   As a member of the Committee on Ways and Means and as a member and chairman of the Committee on Banking and Currency he has exerted a most important influence upon the legislation of the country.

He was the trusted adviser and friend of Chase and Fessenden and Boutwell.   He was a friend and confidant of Stanton and Sumner and Lincoln.   And, Mr. Speaker, I may say that his friendships and his valuable influence extended far beyond the region of his party associations.   He was a friendly man; he was a thoughtful and considerate man.

He could clearly perceive and could clearly express what he thought.   He had none of the graces of oratory, but in the time of his strength he was combative, forcible, energetic in the maintenance of the views which he believed sound.

But, Mr. Speaker, it is as we remember him so recently among us, rather than as the man of business or the politician, that I desire to speak of him to-day.   His modest and simple nature would have shrunk from anything like public eulogy, but his affectionate heart would have rejoiced in everything that spoke of kind and friendly remembrance.   I think that we all of us have felt as we have looked upon that silvered head that whoever else might bear the title by courtesy, Mr. HOOPER after all must be considered as the father of this House.

Possessed of large wealth which enabled him to gratify his friendly tastes, he was the most hospitable of men; hospitable not only in the sense in which many who are men of wealth may exhibit that quality, by costly and frequent entertainments, but by a hospitality and flowing courtesy toward all men.   He attracted to his house and to his society men among the ablest and the best which our country furnishes, and with them men of less note and even sometimes men whom it would require a large charity to reckon of that number.

He had firm convictions; he adhered to his own opinions.   But he had no animosity, and his willingness to receive and treat with fairness the differing opinions of others had nothing in it of the condescension of toleration. He recognized human differences and he had a large catholic spirit which could embrace relations with men of all classes of opinion. Men of fame, men distinguished in science and in letters, have been his friends and associates. And he extended to the poor and the lowly a free and generous liberality which should bring a benediction upon his memory.

When the ear heard him, then it blessed him; and when the eye saw him, it gave witness to him because he delivered the poor that cried, and the fatherless, and him that had none to help him.

His private charities were limited only by his knowledge of the wants of those about him. And in addition to those which he bestowed, and so quietly that except by comparison of the knowledge accidentally obtained, one person with another, few could have any idea of their extent, he employed an almoner to seek out cases of want, whose distribution to the poor of this city has reached to thousands of dollars. He was liberal to public objects, and founded a school of mines in Harvard College with an ample endowment.

I think, Mr. Speaker, he has left in this House no enemies; all of us who knew him were his friends. He has gone from us; and we turn to our public duties more sadly because we miss him from among us.

It has been touching to note during the present session what a change gradually came over him, with his failing strength and increasing years. Formerly taking his full part in social intercourse, exhibiting a ready and genial humor, a promptness to argue any proposition, I noticed that during this session he became gradually more silent, his conversation partaking more and more of reminiscences, and that he became what in the clamor for a hearing so often prevailing in this assembly we have all learned to value—a good listener. He will be long affectionately remembered by those of us who have known him; and he deserves to be honorably remembered for his great public service. His family—wife, children, grandchildren—were all in a foreign land at the time of his death. But there were affectionate and tender friends and relatives about his dying bed; and those who followed him to the grave felt that their presence recognized not only a public loss, but a deep and general private sorrow.

Mr. Speaker, I submit the following resolutions:

Resolved, That this House has heard with deep regret the announcement of the death of SAMUEL HOOPER, late a member of this House from the State of Massachusetts.

Resolved, That as a testimony of respect for the memory of the deceased, the members and officers of the House wear the usual badge of mourning for thirty days.

Resolved, That a copy of these resolutions be transmitted by the Clerk to the family of the deceased.

Resolved, As a further mark of respect, that the House do now adjourn.

ADDRESS OF MR. PIERCE, OF MASSACHUSETTS.

Mr. SPEAKER: I rise to second the resolutions which have just been offered, and to add a few words to what has been said so well by my distinguished colleague [Mr. E. R. HOAR] who preceded me.

Representing in part upon this floor the city of Boston, I regard it to be my duty, as it is my desire, to give expression to the sense of the loss which she has sustained by the death of Mr. HOOPER, who for fourteen years was her faithful and trusted Representative. A son of Massachusetts, Boston had been his home for nearly fifty years, and he was thoroughly identified with her people and her interests. He contributed his full share toward the development of her resources and the promotion of her prosperity and growth. As her Representative in Congress, he sought and succeeded in winning for her the good opinion of his associates from other parts of the country, and did much, I think, to dissipate the prejudices which unhappily too often prevail among our people and color their action.

Few men in public life can point to a longer or more honorable service than fell to the lot of Mr. HOOPER.

In the State legislature he was distinguished for his independence and for the progressive measures he espoused, which were much in advance of the sentiment of the party to which he belonged. His seven terms in Congress covered the most eventful period of our history as a nation. During that time a social and political revolution was accomplished, all the powers conferred upon Congress by the Constitution were brought into exercise, and measures affecting the most precious rights of individuals and States were daily pressed for action. In the determination of these questions Mr. HOOPER acted worthily and ably. The possession of wealth enabled him to extend to others a generous hospitality, and he could count among his friends the most distinguished citizens of our own and foreign countries. From this wide and liberal association he derived a store of varied knowledge of affairs that became of inestimable value in the discharge of his duties in this House, upon which his associates could always depend and from which they freely drew. His judgment had been strengthened and enlightened by long attention to important questions affecting the State and free intercourse with those who made them a study. We can all join, sir, in recalling his familiarity with questions of finance and commerce, and the readiness with which he imparted information concerning them.

Mr. HOOPER closed his career as a legislator in the ripeness of age. Declining to engage anew in the cares and labors of congressional life, he passed away when those cares and labors were for him shading unto their end.   The records of this House attest his usefulness, but by none but those who personally knew him can his generosity and kindness be properly appreciated.

ADDRESS OF MR. NIBLACK, OF INDIANA.

Mr. SPEAKER: There is no time when it is so difficult to find language to express the real emotions of the heart as on an occasion like this. This is due in part doubtless to the confused and stricken condition of the mind which naturally follows the death of one whom we have been accustomed to honor and esteem.   The sad reflections which overshadow us are not relieved by the utterance of any words, however fitly chosen.   Reverential silence seems to be more appropriate.

I cannot speak of Mr. HOOPER as those who have preceded me; it was not my fortune to know him so long and so intimately as they knew him.   My acquaintance with him commenced with the assembling of the Thirty-ninth Congress, in December, 1865.   Before I had the honor of meeting him here I had learned to regard him as one of the most esteemed and trusted members of this House, who had entered Congress during the eventful period of the war, and whose opinions had deservedly great weight with those who were charged with the administration of the Government.   A brief acquaintance with him served to confirm those very favorable impressions which I had already received as to his great worth as a man and his fidelity as a public officer.

Two years later, on the organization of this House in the Fortieth Congress, I became a member of the Committee on Ways and Means, of which Mr. HOOPER was then, as he had previously been, one of the leading members. That brought me into more intimate relationship with him than I had previously enjoyed. My two years' service with him on that committee gave me many opportunities to witness something of his daily life and to judge of the ability and fidelity which he brought with him to the discharge of his public duties.

It was not to be expected that I would always agree with him in measures of public policy. We approached questions here very frequently from different stand-points, and represented constituencies often not in accord in their theories of government. I trust, however, I am none the less able on this account to do ample justice to his character.

While faithful to what he considered the peculiar interests of those he represented, I never found him apparently governed by any narrow or sectional views. Impressing me from the first as a just, discreet, and fair-minded man of broad and liberal sentiments, I came soon to regard him as a model representative of that class of solid and progressive men to which he pre-eminently belonged. So I have continued to regard him.

Kind, genial, benevolent, faithful, industrious, and vigilant, he pursued the right as it was given him to see it with unfaltering steps and unruffled temper. The petty storms which occasionally sweep over this House burst harmless over his head without disturbing that quiet dignity of deportment which always attended him as a member of this body.

While true to his friendships and earnest in his convictions, he carried with him that conciliatory disposition which disarmed all personal antagonism, and if he had a personal enemy among all the members of this House I am quite unaware of it.

It was my good fortune, Mr. Speaker, to have received at the hands of Mr. HOOPER many attentions and courtesies, which have made a lasting impression upon me and which I shall always kindly remember. Indeed, such were the kindly personal relations existing between us for several years past, that I have been accustomed to regard myself as one of his personal friends, and as such I have reason to believe he regarded me.   I unite, therefore, with affectionate earnestness in doing every suitable honor to his memory.

ADDRESS OF MR. BUTLER, OF MASSACHUSETTS.

Mr. SPEAKER: All that the usage or custom of the House of Representatives requires upon such a solemn occasion as this has been done, and well done; and perhaps it were best that here these funeral ceremonies should close.   But to me this occasion is not one of mere ceremony.   Almost a quarter of a century ago I was drawn into the closest relations with Mr. HOOPER in the representative assembly of our Commonwealth; and from that hour he has been to me a friend so faithful, so just, so wise, and so true that I cannot let this last hour of mournful farewell pass without bearing testimony to those great, noble, and generous qualities of mind and heart which distinguished him quite beyond any man I ever knew.   I need not—indeed, I cannot—add a word of eulogium.   It is not my purpose to eulogize my deceased friend and fellow-member, with whom I have served here for eight years in closest harmony and closest friendship. I pray your pardon, Mr. Speaker, and that of the House, in thus possibly contrary to usage giving my heartfelt testimony to the kindest heart and the noblest mind in all the relations of life, that filled with all the best attributes of social intercourse, and which overflowed with charity to all men and the truest loyalty to friendship.

The resolutions submitted by Mr. E. R. HOAR were then adopted unanimously; and in accordance therewith (at five o'clock p. m.) the House adjourned.

PROCEEDINGS IN THE SENATE.

A message from the House of Representatives, by Mr. McPherson, its Clerk, announced that the House had passed resolutions as a mark of respect for the memory of Hon. SAMUEL HOOPER, late a member of the House of Representatives from the State of Massachusetts.

The resolutions were read, as follows:

IN THE HOUSE OF REPRESENTATIVES,
February 20, 1875.

Resolved, That this House has heard with deep regret the announcement of the death of SAMUEL HOOPER, late a member of this House from the State of Massachusetts.

Resolved, That as a testimony of respect for the memory of the deceased the members and officers of the House wear the usual badge of mourning for thirty days.

Resolved, That a copy of these resolutions be transmitted by the Clerk to the family of the deceased.

Resolved, As a further mark of respect that the House do now adjourn.

ADDRESS OF MR BOUTWELL, OF MASSACHUSETTS.

Mr. PRESIDENT: The death and the circumstances of the death of Mr. HOOPER are fresh in the memories of Senators. Mr. HOOPER had three claims of a high character to the consideration of his fellow-men while living, and there remain three special grounds for eulogy now that he has passed away.

In the relations of life that may be called personal he bore himself not only without reproach, but in a manner to command the respect of all who enjoyed his friendship or acquaintance.

He was charitable to the poor in the largest sense of that term; helpful to those who needed assistance either by advice or the use of capital for business purposes; considerate of the wishes, wants, and trials of the humble, and to his friends and associates he tendered an unostentatious hospitality, which literally was without limits.

As a merchant, he was trained, careful, enterprising, and successful. He was one of the oldest and one of the best of the business men of Boston. As an importer, dealing with countries most remote from his own country, he based his undertakings upon a knowledge of the products and the demand for the products of those distant lands. He had knowledge of the systems of finance and currency of other nations, and he was thoroughly instructed in the financial systems of the United States; and this knowledge contributed alike to his success in business and to his success as a representative of business men.

His honorable career as a member of the House of Representatives for nearly fourteen years is known to the Senate and to the country. For many years he was a member of the Committee on Ways and Means, and at different times he was chairman of the Committee on Coinage, Weights, and Measures, and of the Committee on Banking and Currency.

In these various places he brought to the service of the country an amount of knowledge, historical, practical, and theoretical, not surpassed by that of any of his associates. His powers for debate were limited, but his judgment was so highly respected that his